Setting up

Before you start playing, make sure that your keyboard is set up correctly. First, you will need to connect a power supply, either battery or mains. Look at your keyboard manual for how to do this.

Place the keyboard on a table, or a special keyboard stand if you have one. If you are sitting down to play, choose a chair or stool which is the right height for you to see and reach all the keys and buttons easily. If you want to stand up to play, make sure you don't have to bend over the keyboard. Whether you sit or stand, you should be able to hold your forearms horizontally. If you are at all uncomfortable, you won't be able to concentrate.

The band **Pulp**, formed by the singer and guitarist Jarvis Cocker, includes the keyboard player Candida Doyle. It rocketed to fame with the album *Different Class* (1995).

This picture shows the sockets at the back of a keyboard.

The sound usually comes out of loud speakers. Some machines need connecting to a separate amplifier.

On some instruments you can adjust how high or low the notes sound using the tune or transpose features. This can be useful when you play with other people.

The keys on your right play high notes. The notes get higher as you go to the right along the keyboard.

Each key plays a different musical note. Find out more about this on page 5.

Most keyboards run off batteries or mains. You may have to plug the mains adapter into a socket at the back (read the instruction manual for your keyboard).

There is usually a socket for headphones, so you can play without other people hearing. This may also connect the keyboard to an amplifier and speakers, or to a tape recorder.

There may be a socket for a sustain pedal, which lets you make notes sound longer.

There may be a knob that allows you to alter the instrument's pitch (how high or low the notes sound).

Many keyboards have sockets so that they can be connected to a computer, or other electronic equipment, using a system known as MIDI.

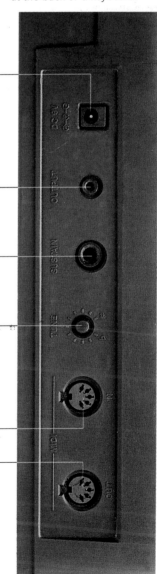

Keyboards use computer technology to make and organize thousands of sounds. To play well, you have to know how to use this technology. Below are some questions about your keyboard which you need to be able to answer before you continue with the book. You may already know some or all of the answers.

If there are any questions you are unsure about, look up the answers in the instruction manual that came with your keyboard. You could also try working things out by pressing the buttons and changing the settings. This is one of the most effective ways of learning about your instrument and how it works.

How do you change the sound?

Some keyboards have a chart of 100 or more sounds (sometimes called tones or voices). You look up a sound and key in its number on a keypad. You can see a chart and keypad on the right.

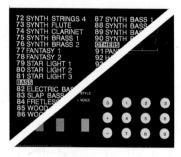

On some keyboards, such as the one on the right, there is a row of buttons, each with the name of a sound. You press a button to select that sound. Instruments like this often have fewer sounds.

Does your keyboard have rhythms?

Most keyboards have drum patterns called rhythms or styles. You can use these to accompany your playing. On the keyboard shown on the right, you select a rhythm by pressing the button next to its name.

On other keyboards you find the name of the rhythm on a chart. Then you press the style button near the keypad (shown on the right) and key in the number for that rhythm. There may be 100 or more rhythms.

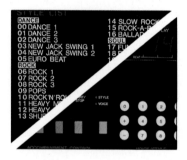

How do you start the rhythms?

Most keyboards have a start/stop button for the rhythms, and tempo buttons to alter their speed. On the right, the up arrow or plus sign makes rhythms faster. The down arrow or minus sign makes them slower.

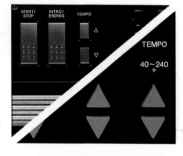

You may be able to set the rhythms to start when you begin playing, using a synchro button. There may be intro/ending and fill-in buttons too, which you can use to vary the rhythm patterns.

Can you use an automatic accompaniment?

Most keyboards that play rhythms can also add notes called accompaniments. Select auto-chord, single-finger (as shown on the right), or the manufacturer's name for your keyboard (check in your manual).

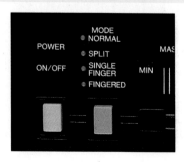

You choose the accompaniments in the same way as you select sounds and rhythms. You control them in the same way too, using the start/stop, tempo, synchro, intro/ending and fill-in buttons.

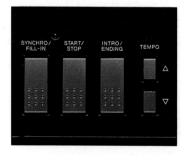

THE KEYS

When you are familiar with the different features of your instrument, take a look at the keys themselves. On all keyboards, the black and white keys are arranged in the same repeating pattern, which you can see on the diagram below. Each key plays a different note. The notes played by the white keys are named after the first seven letters of the alphabet.

As you move to the right along the white keys, the note names go from A to G, then start again at A. In the photograph below, the white keys have the names of the notes they play written on them. For the first tunes in this book, you will only need the white keys. You can find out about playing the black keys later on (see pages 14-15).

Finding notes

The pattern of black and white keys on a keyboard helps you to identify different notes. The black keys come in groups of two or three. You can use these groups to work out and remember the position of the other notes on the keyboard.

Practise finding notes on the keyboard. Think of a letter from A to G. Then, as quickly as possible, press one of the keys that plays that note. Or press one of the white keys at random and try to remember its name as fast as you can.

All the C keys are just to the left of a group of two black keys.

The D keys are always between a group of two black keys.

The A keys are always between the right two of three black keys.

Any two keys with the same name play higher or lower versions of the same note.

C | D | E | F | G | A | B | C

The gap between any note and the next one with the same name along the keyboard is called an octave.

Play any key, then move along step by step until you reach the key an octave above it. Play each black and white key.

How many octaves?

Now you need to work out how many octaves there are on your keyboard. Start on the lowest note, and count the number of notes along the keyboard which have the same name. Most keyboards, though not all, have four or five octaves. All the tunes in this book can be played on a four-octave keyboard, and many can be played on smaller instruments too.

To begin playing the tunes over the page, you will need to find a key called Middle C. This is the key that plays the note C nearest to the middle of the keyboard. The pictures on the right will help you to find where Middle C is on your keyboard. Try to remember where this key is.

If your keyboard has four octaves, Middle C is normally right in the middle.

Middle C

On a five-octave keyboard, Middle C is two octaves from the left end.

Middle C

READING MUSIC

While trying out your keyboard, you can make interesting sounds whether or not you know how to play. But if you want to get the most out of playing, and begin writing your own tunes and songs, it is very important that you learn how to read music. If you can't read music, learning to play is much harder, and passing your ideas on to other people is difficult too.

Born in 1950 in the USA, **Laurie Anderson** uses lots of specially invented electronic instruments and systems in her performances. One of her best-known recordings is O *Superman*.

Lines and dots

Musical notes are written on a set of five lines called a staff (or stave). They can be written on the lines and in the spaces between them. Each note name has a different position on the staff. This depends on a sign called a clef at the start of the staff. A treble clef is usually used for high notes, and a bass clef for low notes.

Because the keyboard can play so many notes at a time, it isn't possible to fit them all on one staff. Keyboard players read music from two staves at once, written one above the other. They usually play the music on the top staff with their right hand and the music on the bottom staff with their left hand.

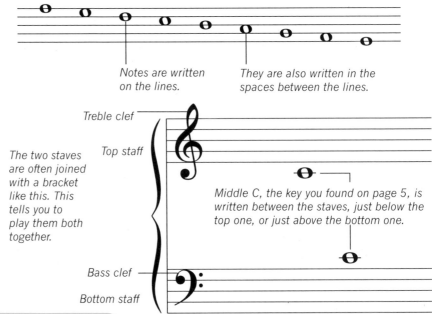

Notes at the top of the staff sound higher than notes at the bottom of the staff.

Notes are written on the lines.

They are also written in the spaces between the lines.

Treble clef

Top staff

The two staves are often joined with a bracket like this. This tells you to play them both together.

Middle C, the key you found on page 5, is written between the staves, just below the top one, or just above the bottom one.

Bass clef

Bottom staff

Finding notes on the keyboard

This diagram shows you how to match keys on your keyboard with notes on the staves. Play each key looking at its written note and saying its name.

As you move along the keyboard, the written notes cross over from one staff to the other. They do this at Middle C.

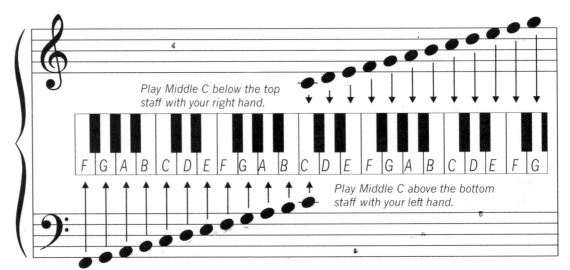

Right-hand notes

Middle C sounds the same whether it is written in the bass clef or the treble clef.

Play Middle C below the top staff with your right hand.

F G A B C D E F G A B C D E F G A B C D E F G

Play Middle C above the bottom staff with your left hand.

Left-hand notes

HOW LONG NOTES LAST

As well as showing you which notes to play, music tells you how long to make each one last. You measure note-lengths in counts called beats. The shape of a note tells you how many beats it lasts for.

A crotchet lasts for one crotchet beat.

A minim lasts for two crotchet beats.

A semibreve lasts for four crotchet beats.

Grouping notes together

When music is written down, it is split into small sections called bars by vertical lines called bar-lines. Each bar contains the same number of beats.

A sign called a time signature tells you how many beats there are in each bar. It comes at the start of the music, just after the clef.

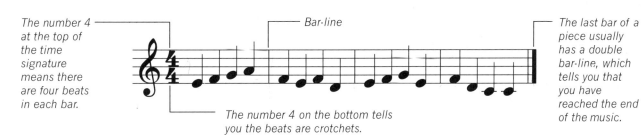

The number 4 at the top of the time signature means there are four beats in each bar.

Bar-line

The last bar of a piece usually has a double bar-line, which tells you that you have reached the end of the music.

The number 4 on the bottom tells you the beats are crotchets.

Starting to play

Try the tune below. First choose a sound that lets you hear what you are playing clearly. Sounds such as *organ* or *piano* are good when you are learning a tune. (There is more about choosing sounds on page 13.)

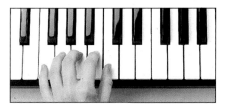

Play the bass-clef notes on the bottom staff with your left hand. You will need the notes C, B, A, G and F.

You need to play some notes with your right hand, and some with your left. The pictures below show which keys you need. Spend some time finding each one before you start to play the tune.

Play the treble-clef notes on the top staff with your right hand. You will need the notes C, D, E, F and G.

Step by step

The time signature in this tune tells you there are four crotchets in each bar. Count "one two three four" steadily, then work out how long each note is. A pattern of long and short notes is called a rhythm.

It might help if you clap the rhythm a few times while you count. Then, when you are familiar with the rhythm, try fitting the notes to it. Don't worry if this seems tricky at first. Keep counting steadily.

The crotchets in the first bar last for one beat each.

Your right hand doesn't play here.

Keep counting groups of four in your head as you play. This will help you know how long to hold each note for.

Your left hand doesn't play at the beginning.

This minim lasts for two beats.

This semibreve lasts for four beats.

LEARNING TUNES

It can take some time to relate written notes to the keys on a keyboard. But the more you look at music and try to play it, the easier it will become. The tunes in this book will help you to learn a little at a time.

If you can already read music, try all the tunes anyway, because they also contain useful hints about keyboard playing. Below, there are some tips that will help you when you start to learn a new tune.

Checklist for learning tunes

- Look at the time signature. Remember, this tells you how many beats to count in each bar.

- Count the beats out loud, or in your head, and clap the rhythm at the same time.

- When you can do this, work out the notes and fit them to the rhythm. Try not to rush, and keep counting steadily.

- Don't worry if you can't do everything at once. Work through the music slowly and it will soon begin to make sense.

Cotton socks

This tune has four crotchet beats in each bar. First count "one two three four" steadily a few times. Then try clapping the rhythm. Keep counting all the time.

Remember to hold the semibreves in bars 4 and 8 so that they last for four whole beats. The first note is Middle C.

Remember to play notes on the top staff with your right hand and notes on the bottom staff with your left hand.

Keep the hand that isn't playing close to the keys.

Try to make the tune cross over smoothly from one hand to the other. Don't slow down.

Rhythms and sounds

To make *Cotton socks* sound more interesting, you can use one of the rhythms on your keyboard, and choose a new sound too. Look in your keyboard manual if you need reminding about how to do these things.

A *folk* or *country* rhythm would work well. Select the rhythm in the usual way and start it playing. Then adjust the tempo until you can play the music over the top. For this tune, sounds like *banjo, acoustic guitar* or *12-string guitar* will be very effective.

Try some other sounds and rhythms too.

Use the tempo controls to set a comfortable speed (not too fast or too slow).

Listen to how the different sounds or rhythms you choose affect the music.

FINGERING

To make your playing sound smooth, it helps to play each note with a different finger from the note before. To help you work out which fingers to use, there are numbers called fingerings above or below some of the notes in the tunes in this book. On the right you can see which finger or thumb each number refers to.

Try the exercise below to help you practise remembering which finger is which.

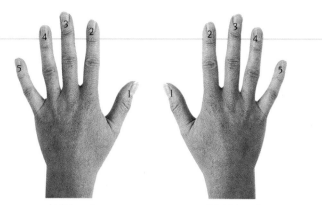

Left hand   *Right hand*

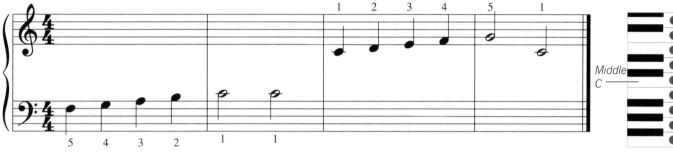

Middle C

First play F below Middle C with your left little finger (5). Play up to Middle C with your left fingers.

Play Middle C twice with your left thumb (1). Lift your thumb in time to play the second C.

Then play Middle C with your right thumb (also 1), and continue up the keys with your right fingers.

You reach G above Middle C with your little finger (5). Then play Middle C with your right thumb.

The diagram above shows the keys you need for the exercise.

Blue valley

Before you try to play *Blue valley*, remember to check the time signature, clap the rhythm, then work out all the notes. Follow the fingerings suggested carefully.

Then try adding a rhythm with three beats in each bar, such as *waltz* or *jazz waltz*. Try a new sound too, such as *flute* or *strings*.

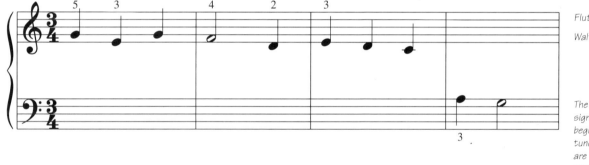

Flute/Strings

Waltz/Jazz waltz

The time signature at the beginning of this tune means there are three crotchet beats in each bar.

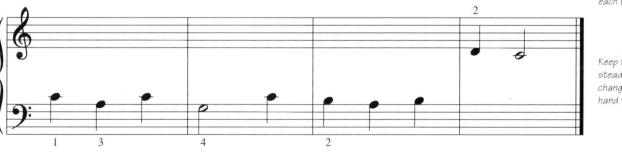

Keep the rhythm steady when you change from one hand to the other.

Playing tips

Next to the tunes in this book, you will find lots of tips and reminders to help you learn. There are also ideas about which sounds and rhythms you could try.

Sometimes there are suggestions about how fast to play (see page 14) and whether you can use an automatic accompaniment (see page 10).

SOUNDS AND SILENCES

As well as sounds, music contains silences too. There are symbols in music called rests that tell you where the silences are, and how long they last. The most common types of rest are shown on the right. When you see a rest, you leave a gap in the music for that number of beats.

A crotchet rest lasts for one crotchet beat.

A minim rest lasts for two crotchet beats.

A semibreve rest lasts for four crotchet beats. (It can also be used to show a rest lasting a whole bar.)

Piece of cake

Watch out for the rests when you play *Piece of cake*. Learn the rhythm first, by counting steadily and clapping. When you play the tune, leave a gap for the correct number of beats wherever you see a rest.

Keep counting the beats during the rests just as you count them for the notes. Take care not to cut the rests short. Remember to follow all the fingerings carefully, too.

Jazz organ/ Trumpet

Funk/Dance pop

Automatic accompaniment (start this by playing the lowest C on your keyboard: you can find out more below)

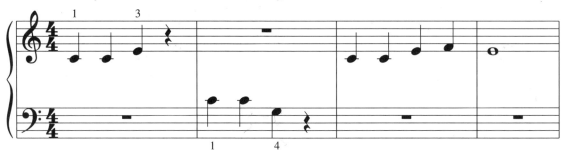

Make sure each crotchet rest lasts for the correct length of time.

Adding an accompaniment

When you can play *Piece of cake* well, you could try playing it using an automatic accompaniment. Turn this feature on in the way you did on page 4. You usually select single-finger, auto-chord, or the setting with the manufacturer's own name. (You can find out about the fingered setting later, on page 32.)

Then find a rhythm that fits the tune. *Funk* or *dance pop* might work well. Start the rhythm playing, and set it at a speed you can play along with comfortably. Then start the accompaniment by playing the lowest C on your keyboard. You will hear other notes begin to play. Count for two bars before you start to play.

Select single-finger or auto-chord, or the special manufacturer's name for the chord setting given in your keyboard manual.

Choose a rhythm and start it playing, then adjust the speed so you can play all the notes easily.

Start the accompaniment by playing the lowest C on your keyboard. It will change depending on which rhythm you select.

Shorter notes

Some notes are shorter than a crotchet. A quaver is half the length of a crotchet beat. Two or more quavers written next to one another are often linked together by a line. When counting a quaver rhythm, it can help to say "one-and two-and three-and four-and", instead of "one two three four".

 One quaver lasts for half a crotchet beat.

 Two quavers last for one crotchet beat. You can count them as "one-and".

╕ *A quaver rest lasts for half a crotchet rest.*

Boil in the bag

Watch out for the quavers and different types of rest in this tune. You could try counting "one-and two-and three-and four-and" for the bars with quavers.

Remember to look at the playing tips next to the tunes. Try the suggested sounds and rhythms, and experiment with others too.

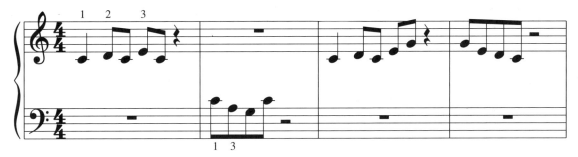

Distortion guitar/ Rock guitar

Rock

Automatic accompaniment (start this by playing the lowest C on your keyboard)

Make sure each rest lasts for its full length. Don't come in early with the next note.

Ray Charles was born in the USA, in 1930. He became blind at an early age, but learned to read and write music in braille.

He began his career playing the piano at nightclubs, but gradually also became known as a singer, keyboard player, composer and arranger. He often played a type of keyboard called a Hammond organ.

Charles made his first recording in 1949, and began to develop an abandoned, passionate style, for example in *What'd I Say*, *Drown In My Own Tears* and *I Believe To My Soul* (all recorded in 1959).

His early influences included R&B and gospel music, which he combined to produce soul music. He is sometimes known as the "father of soul". His songs are performed by musicians all over the world.

Charles has also performed in many other styles, including blues, jazz, country and rock.

DOTTED NOTES

When you see a dot after a note, you have to make the note longer by half as much again. For example, a dotted minim lasts for three crotchet beats. A dotted crotchet lasts for one and a half crotchet beats. The examples on the right show you this.

The next tune contains dotted crotchets and dotted minims. Try clapping it carefully to practise counting dotted notes.

A dotted minim lasts for a minim (two crotchet beats) plus half a minim (a crotchet), or three crotchet beats.

A dotted crotchet lasts for a crotchet plus half a crotchet (a quaver), or one and a half crotchet beats.

O'Leary's cow

Harmonica/ Acoustic guitar

Folk-pop/Pop-rock

Automatic accompaniment (start this by playing the lowest C on your keyboard)

In the second part of this tune, you have to play with both hands together. Practise each hand separately at first. Then play them together.

Both hands play the same note in the last bar of this piece. Press the key with both your thumbs.

TIED NOTES

A curved line between two or more notes on the same line or space of the staff is called a tie. This means you play the first note, and hold it for the same number of beats as all the tied notes added together. Don't play tied notes separately.

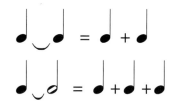

A crotchet tied to another crotchet lasts for two crotchet beats.

A crotchet tied to a minim lasts for three crotchet beats.

Repeats

A repeat sign tells you to play some of the music again. Repeat from the beginning of the piece, or from the previous repeat sign, if there is one. You ignore a repeat sign the second time you reach it.

Repeat from the beginning of the piece or from the previous repeat sign.

Repeat the music between these signs.

Shallow waters

Jazz guitar/ Recorder

Reggae

Automatic accompaniment (start this by playing the lowest C on your keyboard)

A dotted minim tied to a semibreve lasts for seven crotchet beats.

Choosing sounds

Most keyboards make different sounds. Some of these imitate instruments, while others are unusual electronic sounds. Spend time trying out the sounds on your keyboard, so you become familiar with them.

The tunes in this book have suggestions for sounds to use. These are only ideas. You should also try selecting your own sounds. Choosing the right sound for a tune is part of being a good keyboard player.

Checklist for choosing sounds

- When you are learning a tune, use clear sounds such as organ or pipes. These will help you to hear what you are playing very clearly.

- Sounds such as oboe and trumpet last for as long as you hold the keys down. They are good for tunes with lots of long notes in them.

- Some sounds, such as pick guitar or harpsichord, may fade very quickly. They are good for tunes which have lots of short notes in them.

- Distorted sounds, such as metal or bells, can make music difficult to hear, but once you know a tune well, they can be very effective.

BLACK KEYS

So far in this book you have only used the white keys on your keyboard to play all the notes in the tunes. Now you can find out when you use the black keys.

The black keys play notes which are known as sharps and flats. These notes are shown by special signs in the music.

Flats

A flat sign (♭) makes the note after it slightly lower. It also affects any other notes on the same line or space after it in the bar. A bar-line cancels a flat, so a note in the next bar on the same line or space is not a flat, unless it has its own flat sign.

The distance between the flat note and the usual note is called a semitone.

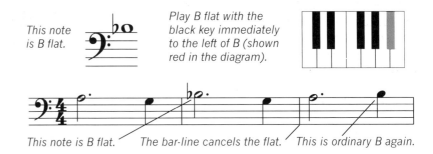

This note is B flat.

Play B flat with the black key immediately to the left of B (shown red in the diagram).

This note is B flat. The bar-line cancels the flat. This is ordinary B again.

Compete!

Choir/Synth

House/Techno

140 BPM (find out more below)

Automatic accompaniment (start by playing the lowest C on your keyboard)

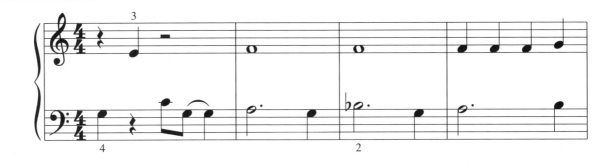

Don't play B flat in bar 4.

Count the tied notes in bars 1 and 5 carefully.

Setting a speed

Next to the tunes in this book, there is often a suggested speed (tempo), in beats per minute (BPM). You adjust this with the tempo buttons. Often a light flashes in time with the beats, to help you count.

Some keyboards have a display which tells you the exact speed at which the rhythm or accompaniment is playing. Or you can work out the tempo roughly in your head. The checklist below gives you some tips.

This display tells you the speed of the rhythm in beats per minute.

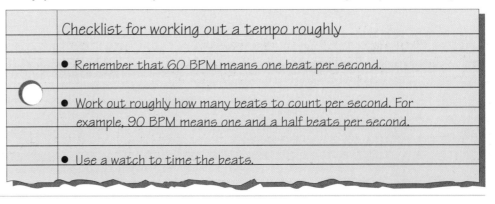

Checklist for working out a tempo roughly

- Remember that 60 BPM means one beat per second.

- Work out roughly how many beats to count per second. For example, 90 BPM means one and a half beats per second.

- Use a watch to time the beats.

Sharps

A sharp sign (♯) makes the note after it slightly higher. Like flat signs, a sharp sign affects any notes on the same line or space after it in the bar. It is cancelled by a bar-line.

The distance between the sharp note and the usual note is a semitone.

This note is F sharp.

Play F sharp with the black key immediately to the right of F (shown red in the diagram).

This note is F sharp.   The bar-line cancels the sharp.   This is ordinary F again.

Holding on

Electric piano/ Strings

Soft rock

118 BPM

(No automatic accompaniment)

Remember, the sharp signs are cancelled by the next bar-line. Don't play F sharp in bars 6 or 14.

Make sure you keep counting steadily during the tied notes so that you don't play the next note too soon.

NEW RIGHT-HAND NOTES

In the next two tunes, there are new notes for your right hand. They are A and B, and C an octave above Middle C. On the right you can see what these notes look like on the staff, and on your keyboard.

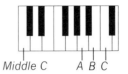

Find these notes on your keyboard. Saying their names will help you remember them.

Take it easy

Piano/Mute trumpet

Cool jazz/Swing

120 BPM

Automatic accompaniment (switch it off to learn the tune, then see below)

Watch out for the fingerings in this tune. Make sure you put your fifth finger on the A in bar 5 and the B in bar 9.

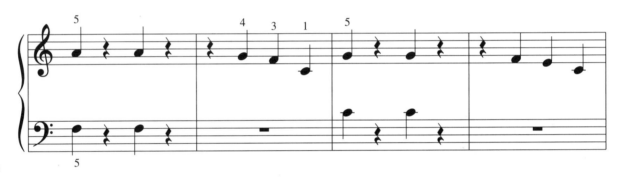

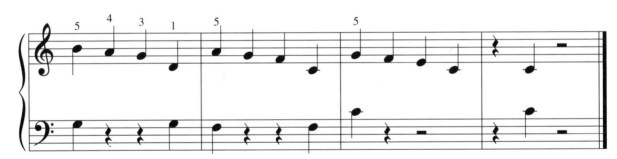

Adding an accompaniment

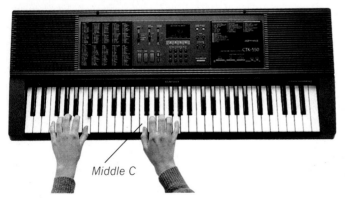

Middle C

To add an automatic accompaniment to *Take it easy*, you have to play the left-hand part an octave lower than normal (as shown on the left). First, learn the tune as normal, with both your thumbs on Middle C. Then choose a rhythm and select auto-chord.

Start the rhythm, then instead of placing your left thumb on Middle C, put it on the C an octave below and play all the left-hand notes in this new position. As you play, the accompaniment part will change, because you are playing in the area of the keyboard where the left-hand notes trigger the automatic chord system. This area is usually marked next to the keys.

USING INTROS AND ENDINGS

If your keyboard has an intro/ending button, you can use this to add a special rhythm at the beginning and end of a tune. Try selecting a rhythm, then pressing the button to hear how the rhythm changes. Experiment using this feature with other rhythms too. The intro or ending changes with each different rhythm you select. If you want to use an intro, listen to it a few times to see how long it lasts, so you know when to start playing.

Select a rhythm, then press the intro button. Start playing when the intro ends.

Press the ending button when you finish, or to accompany the end of the tune.

Taking care of your keyboard

Keyboards are fragile instruments and need to be handled carefully. If you look after your instrument properly it will be much less likely to go wrong.

When you buy a keyboard, it is a good idea to ask in the shop for advice about how to take care of it. There may be some tips in your manual, too.

Checklist for taking care of your keyboard

- To keep the keyboard free from dust, cover it when it is not in use. Make sure you keep it clean and dry, too.

- Keep the keyboard away from too much heat. Make sure you do not place it next to a radiator or in direct sunlight.

- Use a soft duster to clean your keyboard.

- If necessary, use a damp cloth to remove stains, but never use cleaning fluid.

- Do not hit or drop your keyboard. If you have to transport it, use its original packaging or a special carrying case.

- Never take the keyboard apart. If it goes wrong, get help from the shop where you bought it, or from the manufacturer.

Stevie Wonder, from the USA, became blind shortly after he was born in 1950. Despite this, he had learned the piano, drums and harmonica by the age of nine.

His early influences included gospel music and R&B, but he has performed and recorded music in a wide variety of styles, including soul, funk, pop and reggae. He was one of the pioneers of the use of synthesisers, taking full advantage of keyboard sounds, for example in the hits *Livin' For The City* and *Superstition*.

As well as making his own recordings, Wonder has worked as a singer, musician, songwriter and producer for many other performers, including Paul McCartney, Michael Jackson and Eurythmics.

RECOGNIZING NOTES

When you play a piece, it is important to be able to recognize all the notes on the staff quickly, and to know how they relate to the keys on your keyboard. This is so you can play confidently, without hesitating. Several things can help you to do this.

While you play, try to notice whether a group of notes goes up or down the staff, and look out for patterns of notes or rhythms that repeat. Think about the distance between notes too, so your fingers begin to sense where to play.

In the first bar of Flying fish (below), you play the same three-note pattern twice.

In the next bar, there is a similar three-note pattern, but one white key higher.

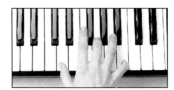

Notice the positions of your right-hand fingers as you play the first bar of Flying fish.

Then keep your fingers in the same position, but move your hand right by one white key.

Flying fish

You can try out some interesting rhythms with this tune, but it sounds best without an accompaniment. Make sure you switch this off before you start to play.

Watch out for the quaver rests in each hand in the first three bars. Remember, each quaver rest lasts for half of one crotchet beat.

Marimba/
Vibraphone

Rhumba/Calypso

128 BPM

(No automatic accompaniment)

In the first three bars, play the left-hand quaver straight after the three right-hand quavers.

Born in 1957 in England, **Paul Hardcastle** has recorded some very popular dance music, using distinctive keyboard textures. In the picture on the right he has his keyboard slung round his neck, so he can dance while playing.

Hardcastle's first major hit was a record called 19 (1985), followed by *Just For The Money* and *Papa's Got A*

Brand New Pigbag.

In 1986 he recorded *The Wizard*, used as the theme tune for the television programme *Top of the Pops*. He has also written other theme music for television.

More recently Hardcastle has worked as a producer for other performers, and has founded his own record label, Fast Forward.

NEW LEFT-HAND NOTES

The tunes on the next two pages use some new left-hand notes: E, D, and the C below Middle C. On the right you can see what these notes look like on the staff, and where to find them on your keyboard.

When you have found these notes, you will know all the white notes from the C below Middle C to the C above Middle C. Play these notes at random and say their names to help you remember them.

C D E

Above you can see what the new notes look like on the staff.

C D E   Middle C

This diagram shows you how to find the new notes on your keyboard.

A good life

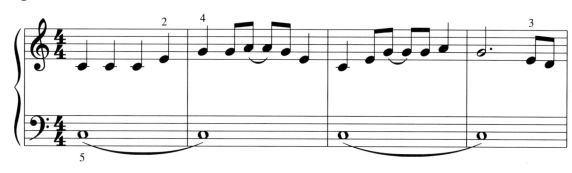

Jazz organ/ Electric piano

Bossa nova

120 BPM

Automatic accompaniment (controlled by left-hand notes)

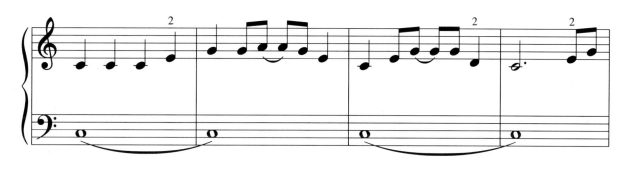

Practise counting the tied rhythm in the right hand. Make sure you don't play the quaver after the tied notes late.

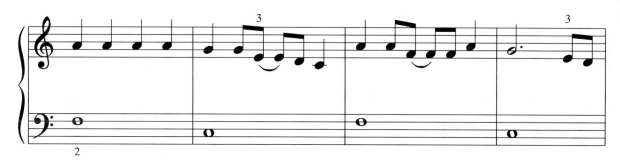

Follow the right-hand fingerings carefully in this tune, especially in bars 4, 10 and 12.

KEY SIGNATURES

One or more flats or sharps at the start of a staff is called a key signature. This tells you to play all the notes on those lines or spaces as flats or sharps throughout the piece. So in *Mind the gap* when you see the note B you have to play a B flat. Key signatures make music tidier and easier to read, because they save writing out lots of flats or sharps.

This key signature tells you to play B flats throughout the piece.

Play this note as B flat.

Mind the gap

Synth bass/Gut guitar

R&B/Funk

124 BPM

(No automatic accompaniment)

Count the rests very carefully in this piece.

Watch out for the fingering in bar 7. You have to move your left hand.

You can find out about adding a fill-in below.

Fill-in

The synchro button

The synchro button makes the rhythm start when you play the first note of a tune (if the note is in the automatic chord area). Select the rhythm, but don't start it playing. Press the synchro button and begin the tune.

Using a fill-in

If your keyboard has a fill-in button, you can use this to add an interesting rhythm during a piece. For example, in *Mind the gap* you could add a fill-in during the rests in bar 4 and in the last bar. Simply press the button.

Changing sounds

You could also try changing the sound or rhythm during the rests in bar 8 of *Mind the gap*. Press the fill-in button, then select your new sound or rhythm as quickly as possible, so you can join in again in the next bar.

Choose a sound and rhythm, and alternatives if you want to change them during the piece.

Press the synchro button, then a key in the automatic chord area. The rhythm will start.

Press the fill-in button in a rest, then move your hand back over the keys.

If you want to change a sound or rhythm, do this quickly during the fill-in, and keep counting.

PRACTISING

There is a lot to take in and remember when you start learning the keyboard. At first it can seem a bit tricky. However, if you practise carefully, the things you learn in this book will quickly become much easier.

Everyone has their own way of practising, but there are some good general rules to follow, which will help you to get the most from your practice. You can read about these in the checklist below.

Checklist for practising

- Make sure you are feeling wide awake and ready to concentrate.

- Choose a time when you are not likely to be interrupted, and when you are not in a hurry.

- Make sure you are sitting or standing comfortably. Your forearms should be horizontal. Keep your shoulders very relaxed.

- Play a tune you already know well at the beginning of your practice. This will help you to warm up your fingers and to feel confident about your playing.

- Clap the rhythm of a new tune before you try playing the notes.

- Learn new tunes slowly at first to avoid making mistakes.

- Practise any tricky bits separately until you can play them well.

- Sometimes, record yourself playing a tune on a cassette. This will help you to listen carefully to how your playing sounds.

- Playing to a friend can help you with your practice too. Only do this when you can play a tune really well.

- Practising a little each day is better than playing for a long time once a week. This will help you to remember the things you learn.

Born in 1960 in England, **Vince Clarke** is a very successful songwriter and keyboard player. He was one of the original members of Depeche Mode, which produced its first hit single, *Dreaming Of Me*, in 1981.

In 1982 Clarke set up a new duo called Yazoo, with the singer Alison Moyet, releasing the successful singles *Only You* and *Don't Go*. Yazoo disbanded in 1983.

After playing with the band Assembly, Clarke went on to form Erasure in 1985 with Andy Bell, which has become especially famous for its spectacular stage-show. Many hits include *Sometimes*, *The Circus*, *Blue Savannah* and *Love to Hate You*, as well as *The Innocents* (1988), *Wild!* (1989) and *Chorus* (1991).

SCALES

Most of the tunes in this book are based on chains of notes called scales. Learning these scales will help you to play the tunes fluently, and to begin writing your own music.

There are many different types of scale. One of the most common is called the major scale. It contains two types of step (or interval) between the notes.

These are called tones and semitones.

On a keyboard, a black key is a semitone from the white keys directly next to it. Two white keys with no black key between them are also a semitone apart. An interval of two semitones is equal to one tone. You can see this in the diagram below. Look at it carefully and find each pair of notes on your keyboard.

There is a semitone between the white notes E and F.

There is a semitone between the black note B flat and the white note B.

There is a semitone between the white note C and the black note C sharp.

There is a semitone between the white notes B and C.

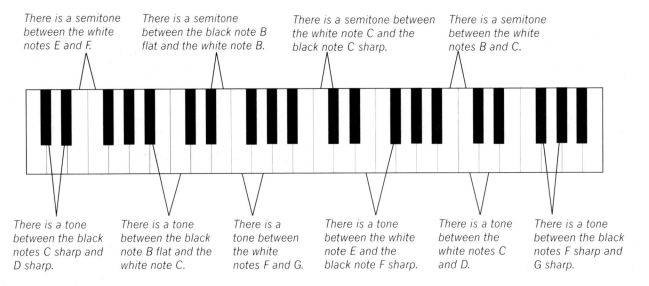

There is a tone between the black notes C sharp and D sharp.

There is a tone between the black note B flat and the white note C.

There is a tone between the white notes F and G.

There is a tone between the white note E and the black note F sharp.

There is a tone between the white notes C and D.

There is a tone between the black notes F sharp and G sharp.

In a major scale, the tones and semitones are always in the same order: tone, tone, semitone, tone, tone, tone, semitone. In a major scale starting on C (shown below) the semitones are between E and F, and between B and C. The other notes are a tone apart.

Major scales are named after the note they begin and end on. So a major scale starting on the note C is called a C major scale. *Scale model* (the tune opposite) is based on a C major scale, and is said to be in the key of C major.

A C major scale does not contain any sharp or flat notes.

In all major scales, except for C major, one or more notes have to be made sharp or flat so that the tones and semitones come in the right order. You can see the scales of G major and F major written out below.

They are both shown twice, once with the sharps or flats written in front of the notes, and once with the sharps or flats written at the start of the staff as a key signature. Try playing them on your keyboard.

In a G major scale the semitones are between B and C and between F sharp and G.

In an F major scale the semitones are between A and B flat and between E and F.

SEMIQUAVERS

A semiquaver is half as long as a quaver. So two semiquavers last for one quaver beat. Four semiquavers last for one crotchet beat. Semiquavers are often joined together in groups by two lines. A semiquaver rest is the same length as a semiquaver (half of one quaver beat).

One semiquaver

Four semiquavers joined together

Semiquaver rest

Scale model

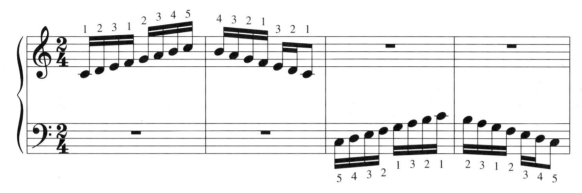

Follow the fingerings carefully: you can use them for many major scales. Don't play too fast at first.

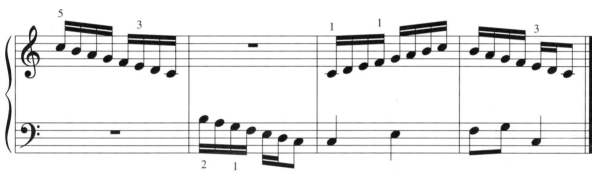

Try to play smoothly. In bar 1, move your thumb under your hand to play the fourth note. In bar 2, move your third finger over your thumb for the fifth note.

In the 1980s, **The Human League** was one of the most successful pop and dance bands. Its recordings were almost entirely based on synthesiser sounds.

The band first became successful in 1981 with the hits *Boys And Girls*, *The Sound Of The Crowd*, *Love Action*, *Open Your Heart* and *Don't You Want Me*. *Dare* (1981) is one of the best-selling albums ever made.

The band has produced new hits from time to time, including *Human* and *Tell Me When*, and the successful album *Octopus* (1995).

MORE RIGHT-HAND NOTES

The next tune contains four new notes to play with your right hand. They are D, E, F and G.

Here you can see what the notes look like on the staff, and on your keyboard.

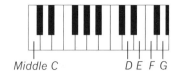

At daybreak

Piano

(No rhythm or automatic accompaniment)

Work out carefully how the left-hand and right-hand rhythms fit together in bar 3. Remember, a dotted crotchet lasts for one and a half crotchet beats.

Herbie Hancock was born into a musical family in the USA in 1940. He learned the piano from an early age, and soon became interested in jazz.

Hancock played with the famous jazz trumpeter Miles Davis for over five years, before setting up his own jazz-rock group in 1968. This played lots of music composed by Hancock, and quickly became very popular. From around this time Hancock began to experiment widely with electronic keyboards and synthesisers.

During the 1970s he turned to jazz-funk, beginning with the album *Headhunters* (1973). This became very popular with disco audiences, and was followed by other successes, including *You Bet Your Love* (1979), and *Rockit* (1983), which show an inventive use of electronic equipment.

In 1986, Hancock wrote the award-winning music for the film *'Round Midnight*, in which he also played and acted. Since then, he has begun to concentrate on jazz again, playing with his own band V.S.O.P. in a passionate style reminiscent of his early performances with Miles Davis.

HOW THE AUTOMATIC ACCOMPANIMENT WORKS

When the automatic accompaniment is switched on, your keyboard registers notes played in the auto-chord area. If you press one key, it selects notes from the major scale beginning on that note. If you play C in the chord area, the accompaniment triggered is based on notes from a C major scale. The main notes used are the first, third and fifth notes in the scale.

Make sure you press only one key at a time in the chord area. If you want to change the chord note, lift your hand before you play the next key.

The main notes which the auto-accompaniment will use if you play the single note C are C, E and G.

Head in the clouds

Synthesiser/Lead synthesiser

70s rock/Heavy rock

132 BPM

Automatic accompaniment (controlled by left-hand notes)

You can press the synchro button to make the automatic accompaniment begin when you start to play the tune. Try using the intro/ending button too.

Some tunes sound better played loudly or quietly, and sometimes you might want to get louder or quieter during a tune. Most keyboards have at least one volume control near the on/off switch. Often there are two separate volume controls, one for your playing and one for the rhythm and accompaniment.

On some keyboards you can also control the volume by how hard you play the keys. These keyboards are known as "touch sensitive". Another way to change the volume is to choose loud or quiet sounds. There are some examples below, but try out others too, to hear what they sound like.

On most keyboards the volume controls are operated by a slider switch.

Sometimes you press an up arrow to get louder and a down arrow to get quieter.

Checklist for loud and quiet sounds

- Sounds such as trumpet, brass and distortion guitar are very loud and strong.

- Sounds such as flute, harp and marimba are quiet and gentle.

Dynamics

The signs below and on the right are called dynamics. They tell you how loudly or quietly to play.

f — Short for forte, which means "loudly"

p — Short for piano, which means "quietly"

ff — Short for fortissimo, which means "very loudly" (louder than forte)

pp — Short for pianissimo, which means "very quietly" (quieter than piano)

mf — Short for mezzo forte, which means "fairly loudly" (quieter than forte)

mp — Short for mezzo piano, which means "fairly quietly" (louder than piano)

The keyboard player and producer **Brian Eno** was born in 1948 in England.

After an early interest in avant-garde music, he joined Roxy Music in 1971. His keyboard style was characterized by very unusual and exotic sounds, which can be heard on the album *For Your Pleasure*.

After leaving Roxy Music, Eno began a solo career, trying out different styles and writing quirky songs. He worked for a while with the guitarist Robert Fripp, with whom he recorded *No Pussyfooting* (1973) and *Evening Star* (1975).

Eno has also worked with many other famous musicians, including David Bowie and U2. He is now chiefly known as a producer, but still records his own music, including *Nerve Net* and *The Shutov Assembly* (both 1992) and *Neroli* (1993). He has continued to experiment with unusual sounds and ways of combining different musical styles.

MORE LEFT-HAND NOTES

The next few tunes contain four new notes to play with your left hand. They are B, A, G and F. There are also some new sharps and flats. Remember, a sharp makes the note a semitone higher and a flat makes the note a semitone lower (see pages 14-15). Look next to the tunes for how to play the sharps and flats.

F G A B

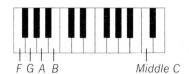

F G A B   Middle C

Practise finding the new notes on your keyboard.

Fool's gold

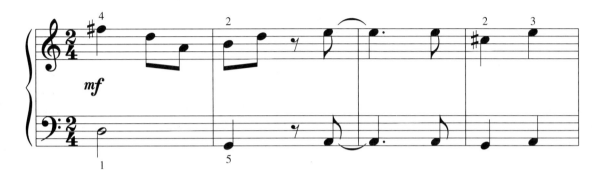

Brass/Guitar

Reggae

124 BPM

(No automatic accompaniment)

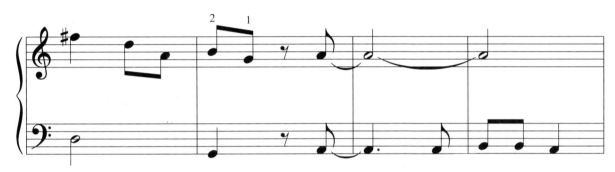

The time signature at the start of this tune tells you there are two crotchet beats in each bar.

The red key in the diagram below plays C sharp.

DEVELOPING YOUR OWN STYLE

Choosing sounds, rhythms, volumes and speeds are all part of developing your own individual playing style. The sounds and rhythms next to the tunes in this book are only suggestions. Keep experimenting with lots of different combinations for each tune. Listen carefully and try to decide which you like best.

You can also use the tunes themselves as starting points for your own new ideas. Start by changing some of the notes or rhythms in a tune as you play, to hear what different effects you can create. You can find lots more advice about making up your own music on pages 34-35 and 40-41.

Me and you

Synthesiser/ Electric bass

Rock

130 BPM

Automatic accompaniment (triggered by left-hand notes)

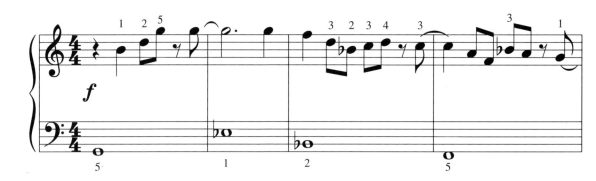

The red key in the diagram plays E flat.

Different fingerings are comfortable for different people. If you don't like some of the fingerings suggested in the tunes, try out your own.

SIGHT-READING

Playing a new piece for the first time is called sight-reading. This can be tricky at first, because you have to read all the information in the music very quickly.

It is very useful to be able to sight-read well, especially when you play with other people. Look at the checklist below for some useful advice.

Checklist for sight-reading

- First, check the time signature. Remember, the top number tells you how many beats there are in a bar, and the bottom number tells you what kind of beats they are.

- Next, look at the key signature. This tells you which notes you have to play sharp or flat throughout the piece.

- Look for any unfamiliar notes, especially any sharps, flats or naturals (see page 31).

- Are there any repeating patterns of notes or rhythms? Noticing these before you start to play can be very useful.

- Choose a steady speed. At first, it is more important to play the right notes than to play the music at the correct speed.

- Count at least one bar steadily aloud before you start to play.

- Keep counting in your head as you play, to make sure you don't slow down or hesitate.

- Try not to stop if you make a mistake.

- Don't worry if you find sight-reading difficult at first. You will find that it gets much easier the more you practise.

Jean-Michel Jarre was born in France in 1948. He started learning the piano at the age of five, and trained as a classical musician, but gradually became fascinated by electronic instruments, especially keyboards.

Jarre's first major recording, *Oxygène* (1977), was a huge success, and was followed the next year by *Equinoxe*. He began putting on huge-scale open-air concerts in Paris, the first of which was attended by over one million people. He has since topped this record with an audience of two million. Some of his concerts have also been shown on television.

Jarre is especially renowned for his spectacular use of laser beams to trigger sounds.

PLAYING CHORDS

In keyboard music you often have to play more than one note at a time with the same hand. This is called playing chords. When you play chords, make sure that all the notes sound at exactly the same time.

If your keyboard is touch sensitive, try to use all your fingers with the same pressure, or one note in the chord will sound louder than the others. This may take some practice, as your fingers have to be fairly strong.

The more you practise, however, the stronger your fingers will become.

In tunes with lots of chords in one hand, you could try using the split keyboard feature, if you have one. This means that the right part of the keyboard plays one sound and the left part plays another. So you could choose a split keyboard sound to make the chords contrast with the main tune.

Starting and stopping

Some pop songs don't have a "proper" ending. Instead, a few bars are often repeated over and over again as the music fades away. There is no firm ending for *Forever and a day* below, so try making up one of your own. For example, when you reach the end, you could play the first four bars of music again.

If you leave out some of the left-hand notes you could use your left hand to fade out the sound with the volume control. Or you could press the intro/ending button for an automatic ending. (Remember, you can vary the automatic ending by using different rhythm settings.)

Forever and a day

Split keyboard: Bass & electric piano

60s soul/Pop

116 BPM

(No automatic accompaniment)

In this piece, the tune is in the left hand. Try out different split keyboard sounds, to find which ones give a stronger sound for your left hand.

A NEW KIND OF REPEAT

In *Fleabitten blues*, there is a pair of bars numbered one and two at the end. They are called first- and second-time bars. The first time you play the tune, play the first-time bar (labelled 1), then go back to the beginning and play the music again. When you reach the first-time bar for the second time, leave it out and play the second-time bar.

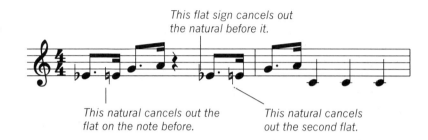

First-time bar   Repeat sign   Second-time bar

Play this bar the first time through the music.

Play this bar the second time through the music.

Naturals

Sometimes, a sign called a natural (♮) cancels out a sharp or flat earlier in the bar or in the key signature. It affects any notes on the same line or space later in that bar, but is cancelled by a bar-line. A sharp, flat or natural sign used during a piece is called an accidental.

This flat sign cancels out the natural before it.

This natural cancels out the flat on the note before.

This natural cancels out the second flat.

Fleabitten blues

Honky tonk piano

(No rhythm or automatic accompaniment)

Remember, the Bs in bar 7 are B naturals, because the bar-line has cancelled the flat sign in bar 5.

MORE ABOUT CHORDS

The pieces on these two pages contain letters called chord symbols. These tell you which chords fit with the tune. The letter C tells you to play a C major chord. This means a chord based on a C major scale.

On the right you can see some of the most common chords based on major scales. Play them a few times until they become familiar.

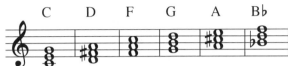

Major chords consist of the first, third and fifth notes of the scales they are based on. So a C major chord contains the notes C, E and G. Try playing the chords below to hear how they sound.

To work out the first, third and fifth notes of a scale, remember the order that the tones and semitones come in (see page 22).

Using the automatic accompaniment to play chords

The automatic accompaniment is very useful for playing chords. Select auto-chord (don't choose a rhythm at first, as this can make it hard to hear the chords clearly). If you play the note C in the automatic chord area, you will hear a C major chord.

This means you can add chords to a tune, by playing the note for each chord in the automatic chord area when you reach the symbol. If you use a rhythm as well, you have to play the note for the chord just before the beat, so that it registers in time.

First select auto-chord. You can choose a rhythm too, when you are used to how chords sound.

Play the note each chord is named after in the automatic chord area of the keyboard.

Your keyboard may also have an automatic accompaniment setting called "fingered".

You select a rhythm and play the whole chord. The keyboard adds an accompaniment.

Margarita

Gut guitar/
Vibraphone

Samba/Rhumba

118 BPM

Automatic
accompaniment
(play the note
each chord is
named after)

Remember to play
the notes for the
chords in the left
hand a little before
the beat, so they
register in time.

MINOR CHORDS

Minor chords are based on a type of scale called a minor scale. Like major scales, a minor scale is named after the note it begins and ends on. But the tones and semitones are arranged differently. The third note of a minor scale is a semitone lower than in the major scale which starts on the same note.

Minor chords also consist of the first, third and fifth notes of the minor scales they are based on, so the third note is a semitone lower than in a major chord. The letter m in a chord symbol tells you to play a minor chord. For example, Am in *Possum city* (below) tells you to play an A minor chord.

On the right you can see pairs of major and minor chords starting on the same note.

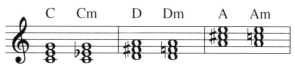

The middle note of the minor chord is always a semitone lower than in the major chord.

Playing minor chords

With auto-chord selected, your keyboard will play a major chord if you play a single note in the chord area. To play a minor chord instead, you usually have to play two notes in the chord area at the same time.

Often you have to play the note in the chord symbol and any note above it. Your keyboard may make minor chords in a slightly different way, so check in your keyboard manual.

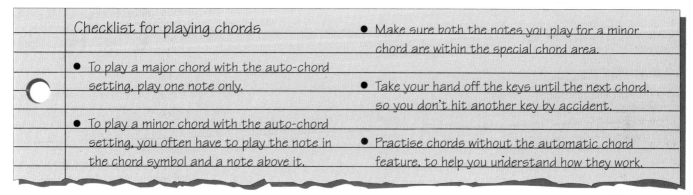

Checklist for playing chords

- To play a major chord with the auto-chord setting, play one note only.

- To play a minor chord with the auto-chord setting, you often have to play the note in the chord symbol and a note above it.

- Make sure both the notes you play for a minor chord are within the special chord area.

- Take your hand off the keys until the next chord, so you don't hit another key by accident.

- Practise chords without the automatic chord feature, to help you understand how they work.

Possum city

Banjo/Accordion

Bluegrass/ Country

126BPM

Automatic accompaniment (play the note or notes you need to trigger each chord)

Count the rhythm in bar 15 carefully, so you know exactly when to fit the semiquaver in.

ADDING CHORDS TO MELODIES

Practising how to add chords to a tune can be very useful if you want to make up some music of your own. If you have a friend who plays another instrument, such as guitar or harmonica, it can be fun to work out accompaniments to their music too.

Select the auto-chord setting, but do not choose a rhythm. Play the melody, adding notes in the chord area with your left hand. Listen to the chords and try to decide which fit best with the tune. This gets easier the more you play and listen.

Chord exercise

Learn the next tune, then follow the steps above to see if you can work out some chords that sound good with it. Don't worry if you find this difficult at first.

The stars above the music are suggestions about where you may need to change to a new chord. If you find some chords you like, write their names down.

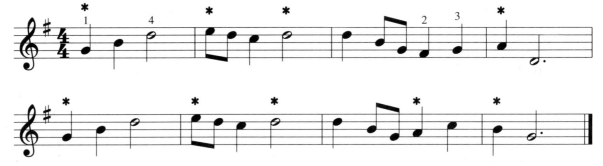

See below if you need a hint about which chords to try using.

You could try using the chords G, C and D. Experiment with using them in different combinations until you find one that you like best.

The sequence G, C, G, D, G, C, G, D, G works well, changing to a new chord at each star written above the music.

Wise guy

Now try adding chords to this tune. It is a bit more complicated than *Chord exercise*. Don't be disheartened if it takes you a while to find the sounds you want. Remember, there are no right or wrong chords to use.

Don't select a rhythm at first, so you can hear the chords clearly. If you want some help to get started, look next to the music for a suggestion. Try adding chords to other tunes in this book too.

Piano/Saxophone

Hard bop/Swing

120 BPM

Automatic accompaniment (use this to work out which chords to use)

The red key in the diagram below plays A flat.

Try using the chords C, F and G.

ADDING MELODIES TO CHORDS

Making up music as you play is called improvisation. One way to begin writing music is to use a sequence of chords and improvise tunes or rhythms over it.

Many bands improvise using a set chord sequence, and copying or imitating each other's ideas. At first try inventing a tune to go with one chord.

Select auto-chord and choose a rhythm. Start with a simple one, such as 8 beat or rock.

Start the automatic accompaniment by playing C in the chord area.

Start to play notes with your right hand. At first, choose notes from the C major scale.

Try to make your tune fit with the accompaniment rhythm. Try using other rhythms too.

Ideas for chord sequences

Try improvising using the chord sequence G, C, G, D, C, G. Play each chord note with your left hand. (You can change from one to another as slowly or quickly as you like.) Choose notes for the tune from the major scale starting on each chord note (D major includes F sharp and C sharp). Some good rhythms to try are *pop*, *rock* and *swing*. Use the fill-in button too.

Changing a tune

Another way to invent new tunes is to adapt one you know. Try playing some of the tunes in this book and changing notes or rhythms. Be as adventurous as you like. This is one of the best ways of finding out what sounds good, and developing your own style.

More starting points

Anything from a picture to a mood can be a starting point for improvising a piece of music of your own. There are some suggestions below. Try lots of ideas.

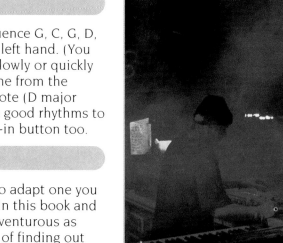

The band **Orb**, formed in 1988 by Dr Alex Paterson, specializes in house music, using keyboards and other electronic equipment to achieve a relaxed, often ethereal, background sound. One of its best-known albums is *The Orb's Adventures Beyond The Ultraworld*, which was recorded in 1991.

The more you try, the more fun improvising becomes. When you find something you particularly like, write it down, or record it on a cassette, so you remember it.

Checklist for starting points

- Listen to music around you for ideas and clues. Think about what sorts of sounds or rhythms you like best, and what you don't like too.

- Think about different types of music. Why does dance music sound different from film music, jingles or ballads, for instance?

- Try writing new theme tunes for television programmes you like. Which sounds and rhythms seem to fit with their stories?

- Try to express some strong feelings in a tune. What makes a cheerful tune sound different from a sad tune?

Born in 1943 in England, **Georgie Fame** began his career as the organist in a band called the Blue Flames. He was an important figure in making R&B and ska styles popular.

His nasal singing style can be heard on the album *Yeh Yeh* (1965), which began a series of hits including *Get Away* (1966) and *The Ballad of Bonnie And Clyde* (1968).

As well as recording some pop songs, Fame has continued to be interested in jazz. He has done a lot of work with the singer Van Morrison, including the album *How Long Has This Been Going On?* (1996).

Something and nothing

Split keyboard: Bass & piano

(No rhythm or automatic accompaniment)

This piece begins on the third beat of the bar, so count "one two" before you start to play.

You need to change the volume at the end of the second line of this piece. Do this quickly with your right hand during the rest.

CHORD MEMORY

If your keyboard has a chord memory, you can programme it to play chords while you play with both hands. You can check how to do this in your manual. You often have to select auto-chord, a rhythm and a tempo. Then you press record and play each chord.

Remember to count each chord carefully. To stop recording, you press start/stop or record again. Then you press play and add in the rest of the music. If you do not have a chord memory, you may still be able to record the chords. Check in your manual.

Other side of town

Electric piano/
Harpsichord

Pop rock/70s pop

126 BPM

Chord memory

Watch out for the minor chords in this tune. You can check how to play them on page 33.

You can use the intro/ending and fill-in buttons when you record the chords if you like. Check in your keyboard manual for how to do this.

SYNCOPATION

One step ahead contains a type of rhythm called syncopation. The right-hand notes don't come where you expect them. There is a quaver rest instead of a note at the beginning of most crotchet beats. The notes come on the second half of the beats. This should not be too tricky when you get the hang of it.

Count very steadily. You could tap a foot on each beat. Play the left-hand part very firmly, and fit the right-hand chords in between the beats. Take care not to slow down. It may help to play this piece with a simple rhythm at first, such as *4 beat*. When you feel confident, you could try more complicated rhythms.

One step ahead

Guitar/Split keyboard: Bass & brass

Reggae/Ska

118 BPM

Chord memory

This piece begins on the fourth beat of the bar. Count "one two three" before you start to play.

If you use a split keyboard sound in this piece, you may find it stops, or "cuts out". This is because keyboards can only make a certain number of sounds at a time. If this happens, try another sound.

The group called the **Pet Shop Boys** was formed in 1981 by keyboard player Chris Lowe and singer Neil Tennant. Its career took off in 1986 with the success of *West End Girls*. Since then the band has produced many hits, including *It's A Sin*, *Heart*, *Domino Dancing*, *It's Alright* and *Left To My Own Devices*. Its music is very inventive, with witty lyrics, lush keyboard sounds and memorable tunes.

Airhead

Distortion guitar

Heavy metal/Hard rock

124 BPM

Chord memory

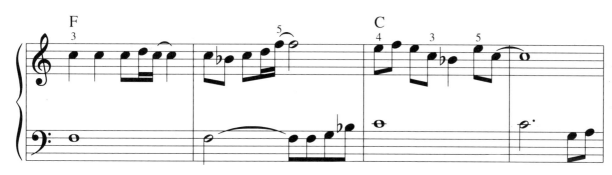

This tune contains some tricky rhythms. It may help if you count quavers (count "one-and" for each crotchet beat).

Count steadily when you play this piece. Take care not to slow down.

WRITING YOUR OWN PIECE

When you have made up or adapted a tune or rhythm of your own, or found a chord sequence you like, try using it as the basis for composing a longer piece.

On this page there are some suggestions for how to do this. Follow the steps carefully, spending plenty of time experimenting.

Starting with a tune

If you have composed a tune you like, you could try to find some chords that go with it, or make up a bass line for your left hand to play at the same time.

Keep listening until you find something you like. You may want to write down chord names or notes, to help you remember them.

Use the auto-chord setting to try out different chords with your tune.

Then add your favourite rhythm track. Does it sound good with your tune?

You could try playing your tune with a bass line and use a split keyboard sound.

Record some chords in the chord memory and play the tune and bass line with them.

Starting with some chords

If you have made up a chord sequence, try recording it using the chord memory, if your keyboard has one. Then play it back and improvise at the same time.

Try to find a tune which sounds good with the chords. You could add a separate bass line too. Use a chord sequence from a tune in this book, if you like.

Thinking about structure

A good structure will help your piece to make sense. Think about how many times you can repeat a tune or chord sequence before it begins to sound boring.

Add variety by playing the same idea in slightly different ways. There are some suggestions below. Listen to the different effects and moods you create.

Checklist for adding variety

- Play the music one or more octaves higher or lower, or start on a different note.

- Try playing your music faster or slower. This may make it sound very different.

- Experiment with sounds and rhythms. Different ones may sound better if you play the music at different speeds.

- Adjust the volume control so the sounds are much louder or quieter. Does this change the mood of the music?

- Try altering some of the notes in the tune when you repeat it, or changing the chords that go with it.

- Try alternating two tunes. Make the tunes contrast with each other, for example in volume or speed.

Beginnings and endings

Think carefully about how to start and end your piece. Try to begin with something interesting, to catch the listener's attention. Try using the intro/ending and synchro buttons with different rhythms to hear what effects you can make.

Thinking about rhythms

If you use a rhythm or automatic accompaniment, think about whether it would be more effective to play it all the time or just some of the time. You could also change the sound or rhythm during the piece, using the fill-in button to give you some time.

HOW THE NEXT PIECE WAS WRITTEN

On the next two pages you will find a dance tune called *Discovery*. Before you play it, read this page and look at the music extracts to find out how the piece was put together, starting from one simple idea.

Then you could try using the same idea to make up your own piece, or start a completely different piece using some of the techniques described below to put it together.

The ideas

① The main idea was a short sequence of notes (riff), played with the left hand.

② This idea was developed by playing the same pattern of notes higher up the keyboard, and starting on the note A, not D.

③ These two patterns were then fitted together. Playing them both at once creates an interesting effect. The new version sounds fairly different from the original riff but, because it is based on the same pattern of notes, it is still recognizable.

④ The second idea was a short sequence of four different chords.

⑤ The chord sequence was developed by playing it very slowly with the right hand, while the left hand played the original riff at the same time.

When you have looked at the music extracts on the right, see if you can find each idea in the music on pages 42-43.

The structure

The sounds build up one at a time.
  The main riff is introduced at the beginning by the left hand. It is played on its own, then with a rhythm.
  The higher version is then added in the right hand.
  The right hand then plays the chord sequence idea while the left hand plays the original riff.
  Then the higher and lower versions of the riff are played in the left hand. The right hand stops playing.
  Finally, the right hand adds the chord sequence over the higher and lower versions of the riff. All the ideas come together, so the music feels complete.
  The ending is based on the rhythm of the riff.

The sounds and rhythms

A *rave* or *house* rhythm at 140 BPM is effective, especially if it is switched off for some of the time.
  The sound changes from *rock organ* for the opening riff to *choir* or *strings* for the second idea, then back to *rock organ*. Fill-ins cover the changes.
  There is no automatic accompaniment.

Rick Wakeman was born in England in 1949. After playing the keyboard for the bands Yes and the Strawbs, he went on to become one of the world's most successful rock keyboard players of the 1970s. The staging of his performances was famously extravagant.
  Wakeman also wrote the music for several films, and recorded the new-age album *Country Airs* (1986). In the late 1980s, he joined the re-formed band Yes for a new tour.

Rock organ;
Choir/Strings

Rave/House

140 BPM

(No automatic
accompaniment)

Learn each hand
separately at
first, then play
them together,
but without the
rhythm. Only
add the rhythm
and fill-ins when
you can play the
music well.

Practise adding
the fill-in and
changing the
sound slowly at
first. It will take
some time to
learn how to
coordinate
everything.

2nd time add
rhythm

2nd time stop playing
and add fill-in

2nd time stop playing,
add fill-in and change sound

2nd time left hand stop
playing and change sound

Count the dotted
and tied rhythm
carefully
throughout the
piece. Make sure
the dotted
quaver lasts for
long enough.

Try to keep
playing at a
steady speed
when you turn off
the rhythm. Don't
slow down.

Turn off rhythm

Re-start rhythm
and add fill-in

Turn off rhythm

PLAYING WITH OTHER PEOPLE

The pieces on the next four pages are for playing with other people. Ask a friend to play the melody part on a guitar or another melody instrument.

The melody is the top line of music in each group of three. Play the other two lines on the keyboard. Follow the tips below to get the most out of playing together.

Checklist for playing with other people

- Learn your own parts separately at first, until you can play them confidently at the correct speed, without making any mistakes.

- Make sure the instruments are in tune with each other. Play the same note together, and listen to hear if each version sounds the same. You may be able to alter the pitch of your keyboard (see your manual), or ask the other players to adjust their instruments.

- Agree on a speed. Play the music fairly slowly at first, to get used to how the different parts fit together. Count a bar out loud before you start.

- Keep counting steadily all the time. Don't slow down or hesitate, as this will confuse the other players. Keep listening too!

- When you have got the hang of a piece, try recording it on a cassette. Listen to how the instruments sound together.

High time

Split keyboard:
Bass & organ

Gospel/Pop

124 BPM

Chord memory

You can record the chords in the chord symbols using the chord memory if you have one. Or ask another friend to play them on a guitar.

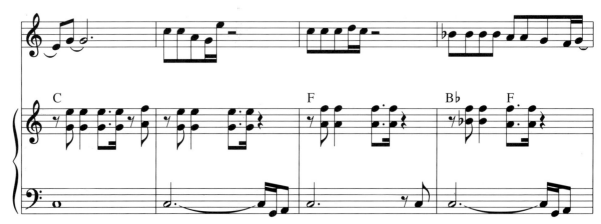

Kraftwerk is a German synthesiser band, producing computerized music. Its sounds are very distinctive, and sometimes eerie. The album *Autobahn* (1974) established its reputation, and it has had a number of hits, including *The Model*, *Showroom Dummies*, *Tour De France* and *The Robots*. Much of its music is dance-based, including the albums *Electric Café* (1986) and *The Mix* (1991).

Take care that the right-hand rhythm in the keyboard part stays very steady throughout this piece. Make sure the dotted quavers and semiquavers last for the correct length of time.

The person playing the melody part has to count and listen very carefully during the rests.

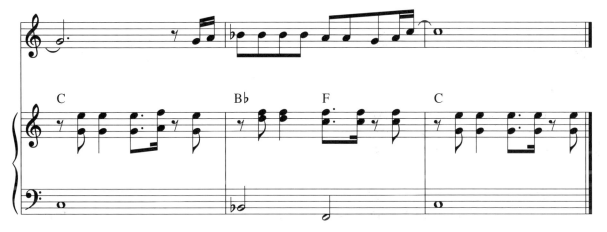

Experiment with using the synchro and intro/ending buttons.

WOODLOUSE

This is another piece to play with a friend. Some of the rhythms are complicated, so it is very important to learn your parts separately at first. You may find it useful to practise clapping the rhythms together.

Look at bars 17 and 18 especially carefully. Try tapping a foot slowly for each quaver beat, and work out which notes you play at the same time as each other. Don't worry if this takes some time to get right.

Synth/Guitar

Funk

118BPM

(No automatic accompaniment)

Work out very carefully how the right-hand and left-hand rhythms of the keyboard part fit together.

Count the ties carefully in the keyboard part at the beginning, and later in the melody line.

You can use a fill-in during the rests in bar 8. This helps to introduce the melody part, which starts in bar 9.

Fill-in

Most of the time in this piece, the keyboard and melody parts play alternately. This means you have to listen and count very carefully in the rests, so you can hear how to fit your notes in with the other part.

Make sure both parts keep playing at a steady speed throughout the piece. Look back at the checklist for playing with other people on page 44 if you need any more tips.

Experiment with using fill-ins during some of the rests. This will help to vary the rhythms.

This piece, and the one on pages 44-45, would be good for playing in front of other people, when you can play them well.

INDEX

Index of tunes

The publishers are grateful to *London Features International Ltd.* for permission to reproduce the photographs of performers in this book.